Peace is

Words by
Annette LeBox

Dial Books for Young Readers
an imprint of Penguin Group (USA) LLC

an
Offering

pictures by
Stephanie Graegin

For Charly, hugs —ALB

For my siblings —SG

DIAL BOOKS FOR YOUNG READERS
Published by the Penguin Group
Penguin Group (USA) LLC
375 Hudson Street
New York, New York 10014

USA / Canada / UK / Ireland / Australia / New Zealand / India / South Africa / China
penguin.com
A Penguin Random House Company

Text copyright © 2015 by Annette LeBox
Pictures copyright © 2015 by Stephanie Graegin

Library of Congress Cataloging-in-Publication Data
LeBox, Annette.
Peace is an offering / words by Annette LeBox ; pictures by Stephanie Graegin.
pages cm
Summary: Illustrations and simple, rhyming text show different ways that peace can be found, made, and shared.
ISBN 978-0-8037-4091-4 (hardcover)
[1. Stories in rhyme. 2. Peace—Fiction.] I. Graegin, Stephanie, illustrator. II. Title.
PZ8.3.L484Pe 2015 [E]—dc23 2013050557

Manufactured in China on acid-free paper

5 7 9 10 8 6

Designed by Lily Malcom • Text set in Fiesole

The illustrations were rendered in pencil and watercolor and then assembled and colored digitally.

Peace is an offering.
A muffin or a peach.

A birthday invitation.

A trip to the beach.

Peace is gratitude for simple things.

Light through a leaf, a dragonfly's wings.

A kiss on the cheek, raindrops and dew.
A walk in the park, a bowl of hot stew.

Peace is holding on to another.

Peace is the words you say to a brother.

Will you stay with me?
Will you be my friend?
Will you listen to my story
till the very end?

Will you wait when I'm slow?
Will you calm my fears?
Will you sing to the sun
to dry my tears?

Will you keep me company when I'm all alone?
Will you give me shelter when I've lost my home?

You might find peace in a photograph,

Or in the deep boom of a belly laugh.

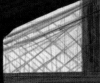

And even in the wake of tragedy,
Even then, you might find her.
In the rubble of a fallen tower.
In the sorrow of your darkest hour.
In the hat of a hero.
In the loss of a friend.

Peace is a joining, not a pulling apart.
It's the courage to bear a wounded heart.

It's a safe place to live.
It's the freedom from fear.

It's a kiss or a hug
When you've lost someone dear.

So offer a cookie,

Walk away from a fight.

Comfort a friend
Through the long, dark night.

Sing a quiet song.

Catch a falling star.

May peace walk beside you
Wherever you are.